Hare's Party
in
Heaven

Dedication

To my wonderful children
Antonia, Noon, Anne, and Nigel
You have inspired me to be the best I could be
Thank you ever so much
I love you forever
To Y and T and all the children who loved listening
to me tell them these stories and who gave me the idea to
record these folktales.
To my mothers; Iscah Oyuga and Rael Owuor and
grandmothers, Sela Tambo (who in old age became
Sheila) Prisca Amos (Nyar Kere), Persila Tambo
who was my lifeline in my childhood, these women
introduced me to Luo folktales.

Hare's Party
in Heaven

Dani Tegan

First published in July, 2020

2nd Ed, December, 2020

ISBN: 978-1-7352657-2-8

∞

Invitation to the Party in Heaven

Once upon a time, there was a king who lived in Heaven. He had a very beautiful daughter. Hare once saw her and expressed his love for her. The king decided to invite him to a party in Heaven because he was a *prospective* son-in-law. The Hare in turn invited other animals to accompany him to the party.

The Hare was the party organizer and the contact for travel arrangements as well as coordinating with the hosts in Heaven.

The hosts asked the Hare to make a list of all animals who would attend the party.

Hare also made a plan of how they would sit on arrival in heaven and a plan of how they would be welcomed and served meals.

*Prospective-something likely to happen at a future date

Preparation for the party in Heaven

Three days before the party the Hare called all animals to a meeting and informed them that the host was looking forward to receiving them. He told them that the host had asked him to divide the group into two for purposes of organizing the party.

Group one was named as "In-laws", and group two was "All of you".

The Hare told the animals that when the host called for "The in-laws," only he who would respond.

But when the host called for "All of you" then all the other animals would respond.

The Day of the Party

On the day of the party, all animals *congregated* at the meeting point near the Hare's home in the early hours of the morning. The flying birds agreed to transport all non-flying animals to Heaven.

The Hawk, the Eagle, and all flying birds made several trips from Earth to Heaven and back to transport all animals to the door of Heaven.

At the door of Heaven, the animals waited to be invited in by the Head Angel.

This was the angel who organized all parties for the king.

The Head Angel arranged the animals into the two groups as Hare had planned. So only the Hare was in the first group named "In-laws". The rest of the animals were in the second group named "All of you".

*Congregated means the animals gathered into a crowd in one place.

Welcome to Heaven

"Welcome in-laws" the Head Angel called out to the animals that had arrived for the party. "Please come in", he added. Hare stepped forward alone. He was escorted by the Head Angel to a big *lavishly* furnished room with a private bath and was invited to freshen up before the big evening party.

Lavishly furnished means furnished in a luxurious manner

The Head Angel then went back to the door of Heaven and said "Welcome 'All of you'. "Please come in."

He then led all remaining animals to a large room. The room had many small wooden chairs and only three bathrooms. In each bathroom there was a shower and a toilet.

The Head Angel invited them to freshen up before the evening party.

The animals hurried to the showers to freshen up. Their room was much smaller than Hare's. Since they were many not all of them were able to freshen up before the evening party.

After a short while the Head Angel knocked on their door and asked them if they were ready because Hare was ready and waiting for them. The Lion replied, "No, half of us are still waiting to shower." The animals started whispering among themselves asking, how Hare was able to get ready so quickly. The Eagle offered to fly out and see what was going on. Soon he returned. He perched on one of the stools and started shaking his head from side to side said "You will not believe this, Hare has a room much larger than ours with a huge bed and a big shower, all for him only!"

The animals became very unhappy. They started complaining asking why they were being treated differently than the Hare. Some wanted to go and see for themselves but the Lion who had become their self-appointed leader told them, "My friends let us be patient, may be it was a mistake" All animals respected and feared the Lion so they kept quiet.

Favours for the In-Laws only

Just before the evening party, the Head Angel went to the room where the Hare was resting and escorted him to the high table. A huge *banquet* had been prepared with so much food piled on the table. One could only see the tip of Hare's ears after he sat down but not his body.

The Hare,
the King and his daughter sat
at the high table and feasted to their fill.
Hare ate, and ate, and ate, until he could barely stand up.

* Banquet is a formal large meal or feast

When he was full, Hare asked the Head Angel to help him
to stand up and to escort him to his room so he could take
a nap. As he was being escorted to his room, they passed
by the room where the other animals were waiting.

The animals were surprised to see that Hare's
belly was so *distended* that he could barely walk.
They stared at him, mouths agape as he walked by with
difficulty. Their own stomachs were empty and rumbling
because of hunger. Hare walked slowly to his room, fell on
his bed and immediately fell asleep.

  * *Distended means swollen*

Other animals hungry and unhappy

The other animals were hungry and wondered why they were not being fed. Before long the Head Angel called out, "All of you please proceed to the dining room." All the animals rushed into the dining room. When they reached the dining room the Head Angel told them, "It is now your turn to eat, enjoy your dinner". They noticed that the food was the leftovers from the high table.

The animals got very angry because of being given leftovers.

But they had no choice but to eat as they were very hungry after the long trip from earth. The female animals served themselves first followed by the male animals.

As they ate, they grumbled because of the bad treatment they had received.

After eating the leftovers, they were ready for the evening party. It was the last activity after which they would leave to return home to earth. However, the animals were still hungry so they decided that they would teach Hare a lesson for having tricked them. Some animals suggested they push hare at the door of Heaven so that he falls down to earth. Other animals felt that he might die and they would then have killed him and they did not like that. The Leopard suggested that instead of pushing him, they could just leave him behind. All animals agreed that that was a better punishment. The birds agreed to leave him behind.

The Plan to leave Hare in Heaven

At the party the Hare was escorted to the dance floor by the Head Angel and after a while he called all the other animals to join him. All animals joined on the dance floor, but they were very unhappy as they were still hungry and tired as they had not taken a nap but they danced anyway.

The birds started planning how they would leave Hare in Heaven. The Eagle being the leader of flying birds decided to organize how they would leave Hare behind.
He wrote a note on a piece of paper saying "birds meet in the rest room".

The note was circulated among all the birds only. The birds left the party saying they were going for a short call. They met in the rest room and planned on how to leave Hare behind in Heaven. They decided that they would tell him that he will be the last to be flown back to earth so as to give him enough time to bid his hosts goodbye. They agreed that the Eagle would be the one to fly him back to earth. The birds agreed not to

Hare jumps down to earth

The Eagle never came back for Hare! After waiting until mid-night, the hosts closed their gates. Hare stood outside waiting at the door. He was sure that the Eagle would come for him.

However, as the night got darker, it became very cold. So, Hare decided to jump down to earth. He fell, and fell, and fell and landed with a THUD on a dirt road in Sondu. It was early in the morning and the sun was just rising.

* A thud is a heavy sound, like that made by a heavy object falling to the ground.

Before long the sun was out, and it started heating up. It was a market day and there were many vehicles driving on the road. The vehicles ran over Hare flattening his body. As the sun got hotter, Hare's body, now completely flattened, dried up. It looked like dried meat known as *aliya* which is a delicacy among the Luo people.

A woman picks up *aliya*

On market days, many women left their homes early in the morning to go to the market, which was about three kilometers away. That day, Min Anyango was one of the first women to reach the market. She had already finished shopping and was on her way back to her home.

As was common in those days, Min Anyango carried her two daughters Atieno and Anyango to the market. The younger one, Atieno, was three years old while the older one, Anyango, was four years old.

Atieno was on her back while Anyango was on her head sitting in the *atonga* (a hand-woven basket). The atonga was also half filled with maize.

On this market day, she had not had money to buy meat.

So, when she saw the *aliya* on the road, she happily picked it up and put it in the basket on her head.

She was happy that she would be able to make meat stew for her family. She continued walking along the roadside happily greeting all the people she met along the way.

Suddenly Anyango screamed
saying "Mama! Meat is
taking my shoes".
Anyango was
known to be playful.
So, her mother rarely took
her seriously. She said,
"Anyango! stop joking,"
"How can meat take your
Shoes?" she added,
"we will soon be home
 and you can go and play.
I know that is what you want."

Min Anyango continued walking happily singing as she went
along.

"Meat" steals Anyango's clothes!

"Mama! Mama! The meat is taking my clothes," Anyango cried out again even more loudly.

Mother was now becoming angry with Anyango. She responded saying, "Anyango! I will deal with you when we get home, stop moving in the *atonga!* You are making it difficult for me to walk quickly. How can you say that meat is taking your clothes? I know you are tired. But we are near home. You will soon be out of the *atonga* and free to run around. So stop *fidgeting* up there!."

Soon, they reached their home. min Anyango passed the gate and was met at the door by her husband, wuon Anyango. He reached for the *atonga* as min Anyango bend down slightly to unload it from her head.

Suddenly, the Hare jumped out of the basket and ran out of the house. Hare was wearing Anyango's clothes and shoes!

* *Fidgeting means making small movements*

The naked child

Min Anyango was *startled.* She dropped the *atonga* as her husband took a step back. The maize poured out of the basket. Wuon Anyango quickly helped min Anyango to untie Atieno from her back.

"Mama! Mama! Mama!" Anyango screamed. Min Anyango reached out and picked up her daughter. She realized that Anyango was completely naked. "Oh my dear daughter," she wailed "What have I done? I should have listened to you! The *aliya* really took your clothes! What has the world come to?"

* *To startle is to cause a person to feel sudden shock or alarm*

Min Anyango used the Maasai *shuka* that had been holding Atieno on her back to cover Anyango who was now *whimpering* quietly. She put Anyango on a chair and together with her husband they picked up all the spilled maize.

Wuon Anyango was at a loss.

All he could say was

"I never thought I would

see a day when *aliya* would

wake up, and steal

a child's clothes. I wonder

where it will go with

such beautiful girls'

clothes and shoes.

* *Shuka means fabric*
Whimpering means to cry or sob

Thu! Atho! Tinda!

The End of Book I

The Hare
&
Animals Party in Heaven

Hope you enjoyed...come back and follow the Hare's
adventures as he goes to show-off his new clothes and
shoes to other animals